LEGO DC COMICS SUPER HEROES

SPACE JUSTICE!

STORY BY TREY KING
ILLUSTRATED BY
SEAN WANG

SCHOLASTIC INC.

WHEN THE WORLD IS IN TROUBLE, IT CAN COUNT ON HEROES TO SAVE THE DAY!

WHEN LEX LUTHOR AND GORILLA GRODD TEAM UP, SO DO SUPERMAN AND BATMAN. THEY WORK TOGETHER TO TAKE DOWN THE VILLAINS AND HELP THOSE IN DANGER.

BETWEEN MISSIONS, THE HEROES HANG OUT AT THEIR SECRET HEADQUARTERS. WHEN THEY AREN'T FIGHTING BAD GUYS, THEY LIKE TO HAVE FUN.

SUPERMAN AND BATMAN NEED A DAY OFF.
THEY LEAVE THE OTHER HEROES IN CHARGE.

HAS ANYONE SEEN MY BEACH UMBRELLA?

"IF THERE'S AN EMERGENCY, REMEMBER: IT'S NOT ABOUT WORKING FAST, IT'S ABOUT WORKING SMART!" SUPERMAN REMINDS THEM.

THE HEROES' MOVIE IS CUT OFF BY A MESSAGE FROM THREE SPACE SUPER-VILLAINS: DARKSEID, SINESTRO, AND BRAINIAC. "WE WILL ATTACK YOUR PLANET—UNLESS EVERYONE ON EARTH SENDS US ALL THEIR TOYS. YOU HAVE 24 HOURS!"

ALL OF OUR TOYS?! THOSE VILLAINS!

THE VILLAINS ARE TOUGHER THAN THE HEROES THOUGHT. ARROWS CAN'T GET THROUGH SINESTRO'S SHIELD. DARKSEID IS AS STRONG AS SUPERMAN.

AND BRAINIAC IS . . . WELL, BRAINY! THE HEROES DIDN'T STAND A CHANCE WITHOUT A PLAN.

WORKING TOGETHER, THE THREE HEROES COME UP WITH A VERY SMART PLAN.

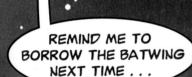

THE THREE HEROES FLY OFF TO OUTER SPACE TO SAVE THEIR FRIENDS, THE WORLD, AND—OF COURSE—ALL THE TOYS!

BATGIRL PUTS ON A DISGUISE. THEN SHE KNOCKS ON THE DOOR AND DELIVERS A MYSTERIOUS BOX TO DARKSEID.

SPECIAL DELIVERY.

FOR ME?!

THIS END UP

WHEN THE SPACE ALIEN OPENS THE BOX, HE GETS A HERO-SURPRISE. EVERYTHING IS GOING ACCORDING TO THE PLAN.

NEXT, SUPERGIRL PUTS A SHEET OVER HER HEAD AND SNEAKS UP ON SINESTRO. WHEN HE GETS SCARED, HIS RING LOSES POWER.

AFTER THAT, WONDER WOMAN TAKES CARE OF SINESTRO. NOW THE OTHER HEROES ARE FREE. "WHAT A GREAT COSTUME!" SAYS HAWKMAN.

"WHAT A GREAT PLAN!" SAYS GREEN ARROW.

THE HEROES HAVE BEEN SAVED AND THE VILLAINS HAVE BEEN DEFEATED ALREADY. "WAIT A MINUTE," SAYS SUPERGIRL, "WEREN'T THERE *THREE* BAD GUYS?"

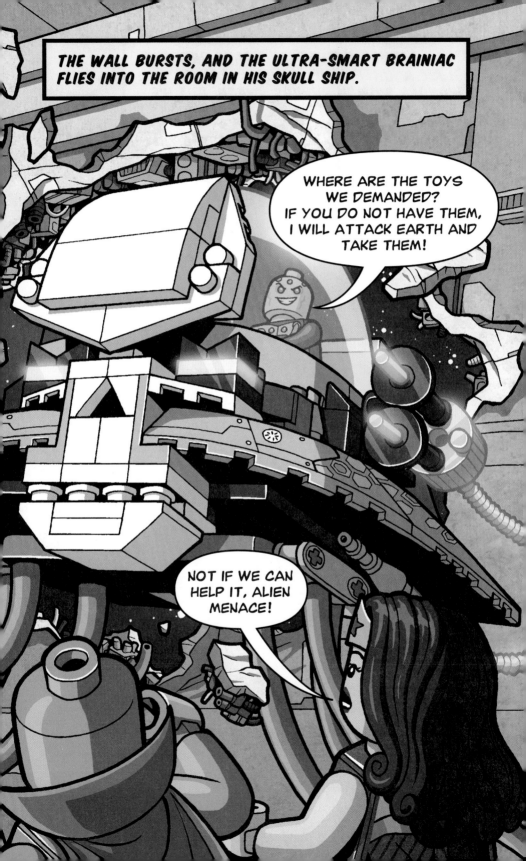

THE HEROES WORK TOGETHER—USING THEIR BRAINS AND MUSCLES AGAINST BRAINIAC!

"ALL I WANTED WERE TOYS," BRAINIAC SAYS. "IS THAT SO WRONG?"

GREEN LANTERN USES HIS POWER RING TO FLY THE VILLAINS TO SPACE JAIL.

"ARE THERE TOYS IN SPACE JAIL?" DARKSEID ASKS. "ONLY IF YOU BEHAVE," GREEN LANTERN ANSWERS.